PARTY GIRLS

Lauren's Spooky Sleepover

PARTY GIRLS

Lauren's Spooky Sleepover

Jennie Walters

illustrated by Jessie Eckel

h

Hodder
Children's
Books

a division of Hodder Headline Limited

For Mary-Kate and Maggie in Bethlehem, PA

A Catalogue record for this book
is available from the British Library

ISBN 0 340 79591 3

Typeset by Hewer Text Ltd, Edinburgh
Printed and bound in Great Britain
by Guernsey Press

Hodder Children's Books
a division of Hodder Headline Limited
338 Euston Road
London NW1 3BH

FACT FILE: LAUREN

Full name: Lauren Danielle
  Turner
Nickname: Laurie
Family: mum Valerie, dad
  Daniel, loads of cousins!
Star sign: Scorpio
Hair: black
Eyes: dark brown
Likes: making things, reading, drawing,
  decorating my room
Dislikes: meat, having asthma, cold rainy
  days
Favourite food: pasta
Favourite pizza topping: onion,
  mushroom and olives
Favourite thing in
  your wardrobe: purple
  tie-dye T-shirt
Ambition: to be a designer
Worst habit: daydreaming
Best quality: being creative

'Wake up, Miss Turner! You're not listening to a word I'm saying, are you?'

Lauren gave a start at the sound of her teacher's exasperated voice. It was true: she'd been staring out of the window, wondering whether her black trousers would look cool if she put star studs down the legs.

'Sorry, sir,' she muttered, feeling rather sheepish. Mr Maclaren had only been teaching the class for a couple of weeks, since the start of that September term, and Lauren didn't want to get in his bad books already.

'I suppose it's no good expecting you to answer the question, then?' Mr Maclaren asked in a resigned tone of voice, taking off his glasses and wiping them on a red spotty handkerchief.

1

Lauren racked her brains desperately, in case the question had somehow floated into her head while she was thinking about other things and was waiting for her to pay it some attention. No such luck.

And then, to her huge relief, there was a knock at the door and one of her best friends, Jess, appeared from the other classroom down the corridor. 'Sorry to bother you, but Mrs Thomas says have you finished with the key to the art cupboard?' Jess asked Mr Maclaren. 'She needs it back now.'

'Oh, good heavens! Yes, I have,' he replied worriedly, searching through the piles of books, pens and papers all over the table. 'Where on earth is it?'

A buzz of conversation and activity broke out in the class while their teacher was distracted. Melissa Wilkins unwrapped a stick of chewing gum and Jess's twin brother, Matt, pulled a face at her. Ignoring him, Jess winked at Lauren (who was sitting at the nearest table) and dropped a small square of folded paper on to her lap.

'Here we are!' Mr Maclaren announced triumphantly, pulling the key out of his pocket and handing it over. 'Tell Mrs Thomas I'm sorry about the delay, will you, Jessica?'

'Yes, sir,' Jess replied with a cheesy grin. She made for the door, sticking her tongue out at Matt on the way.

Lauren unfolded the note under the table, propping her head on one hand to shield the fact that she was looking down. Jess's scribbled writing was hard to read, but eventually she worked it out.

Meet you by the dustbins at break. Sunny's had an e-mail from Nikki! Pass this on.

Lauren knew exactly who she was meant to pass the note on to: Michelle or Caz, her two best buddies in the class. Lauren, Michelle, Caz, Sunny and Jess hung around together all the time, and they always met up behind the school kitchens when there was anything important to discuss.

Their other best friend, Nikki, had moved to California at the beginning of that term. Lauren

3

still couldn't get used to her not being there. She'd known Nikki most of her life – since nursery school, anyway – and things just weren't the same without her. They'd each had a postcard from Nikki ten days ago to say that she'd arrived and San Diego was 'awesome' but since then, nothing. Lauren couldn't wait to discover whether she was happy and had made any new friends.

San Diego

Oh well, she'd find out soon enough. In the meantime, she had to work out how to get this note to Michelle without Mr Maclaren noticing – or Melissa, who was sitting between Lauren and Michelle and poked her nose into everything.

Mr Maclaren had arranged all the tables in their classroom in rows and – for some strange reason known only to teachers – had made everyone sit in alphabetical order, according to their last name, going backwards. That meant those at the end of the alphabet were sitting at the front, right under his nose. Lauren was

4

between Becky Smith, the class boffin, and Melissa Wilkins, the class bully. OK, her friend Michelle (Williams) was only one seat further on, but Melissa was a big obstacle between them. And Caz (Bennett) was miles away at the back of the class.

Luckily, just at that moment Melissa dropped a pencil on the floor. Lauren checked to see whether Mr Maclaren was looking, then hastily sent the note skidding across the tables to Michelle. Phew! Made it . . .

'Oh, she's so lucky!' Michelle sighed that breaktime, passing Nikki's e-mail on to Caz. The paper Sunny had printed it out on was already creased and tattered round the edges from having been pored over so often. 'Can you imagine having your own private swimming pool?'

Lauren leant over Caz's shoulder to read what Nikki had written.

Dear Sunny, and everyone else!
Well, here I am, living in San Diego. It feels so weird, as if we're just on holi-

day here for a while. You should see our house – it's great! There's a swimming pool in the back garden (sorry, yard!) and my bedroom is huge. The wardrobe (closet!) is so big you can walk into it. Eat your heart out, Miche!

I've started at Lincoln Elementary School. It's OK so far. The work isn't too hard, and there's loads of sport – swimming, gym and American football (naturally!). Everyone's making a big fuss of me because I'm new and from England. (You're right – they do want to hear my accent the whole time!) The school's much bigger than Greenside, so I keep getting lost. I haven't really made any friends yet but the two girls sitting next to me seem quite nice – Lisa and Belle. Guess what? There's another girl called Nancy who looks <u>exactly</u> like Melissa Wilkins! Spooky or what? I'm steering clear of her in case she turns out to act like Melissa too.

Better go now. Write or e-mail me soon -
PLEASE! I miss you all loads. How are
Frankie and Fred, Jess? Don't give them
too many sunflower seeds, will you?

Tons of love,
Nikki
XXXXXXX

'I think she sounds a bit lonely,' Caz said, when
they'd both finished. 'I know what it's like,
remember? Starting all over again at a new
school where everyone else has made friends
already and you're the odd one out.'

Caz had only been a part of their gang for six
months or so, since the Easter holidays when
she'd moved in next door to Lauren. At first,
they'd all got completely the wrong idea about
her – partly because Melissa had taken Caz
under her wing when she'd first arrived and
hadn't let her make friends with anyone else.
Now, though, Caz and Lauren were in and out of
each other's houses the whole time.

'And look what happened to you,' Jess

grinned, ruffling Caz's blonde hair. 'You struck it lucky and met us! Nikki's bound to make friends sooner or later.'

'Frankie and Fred *are* all right, aren't they?' Lauren asked Jess. (She was looking after the two rats for Nikki until she came back from the States.) 'They're not pining away?'

Jess was a real laugh but she wasn't the most reliable person in the world. Lauren could imagine her forgetting to feed the rats, or letting them out of the cage to play and then losing them somewhere. She'd have taken Frankie and Fred herself, but their fur or their bedding would probably have set her asthma off.

'No, they're fine,' Jess reassured her. 'I'm waiting on them hand and foot.'

Lauren took another look at the e-mail and sighed. She definitely wouldn't have fancied leaving all her friends behind, but there was something exciting about the idea of living in a foreign country. Especially America – and California, too! Her mum was American, so they

8

went over to the States nearly every year to visit the family. That was in New York, though; Lauren had never visited the West Coast.

'Hey, Sunny,' Caz said suddenly, 'can you come round some time and show me how to e-mail Nikki back? Mum's bought a computer for us to have at home, now she's working, and we got linked up to the Internet last night.'

'Sure,' Sunny said, stuffing the e-mail back in her pocket. 'There's nothing to it, once you've got her address on your system.'

'Hey, look!' Jess broke in, pointing at the staffroom window opposite which they could just see from their hiding place. 'There's Taffy Thomas, talking to Mr Mac. I bet she's giving him a hard time about the artwork key. She was really mad this morning!'

'Yep, looks like he's grovelling,' Lauren said, peering over her shoulder.

'Mrs Thomas is so stressed out!' Sunny put in. 'She's always losing her temper about the slightest little thing.'

'Well, you had Miss Gibson last year, and she's just about the nicest teacher in the whole school,'

Michelle said to Sunny and Jess, popping open a bag of crisps and passing them round. 'Now it's your turn to suffer. Fair's fair.'

'How are you getting on with Mr Mac?' Jess asked, digging into the bag.

'Oh, he's really nice!' Caz replied. 'I think so, anyway. Mum heard from somebody that this was his first proper teaching job.'

'He's so old-fashioned, though!' Michelle said. 'He dresses like an old man. Those waistcoats – and the corduroy trousers! Sad, or what?'

'I like him,' Lauren said stoutly, still feeling guilty about that morning's lesson. 'I just wish he hadn't made us sit in alphabetical order, that's all. I can't stand being next to Melissa! She's always trying to copy my work and sneering at my clothes or my hair, or the way I write. And she tipped a jar of pencils off the table yesterday and tried to make out I'd done it.'

'Tell her to get knotted!' Jess advised. 'She only picks on you because she knows you won't fight back.'

'Yeah, she doesn't try it on with me,' Michelle

snorted, screwing up the empty crisp packet and shoving it back in her pocket. 'You've got to stand up to her, Laurie!'

'I suppose so,' Lauren replied, pulling a face. The trouble was, whenever she tried to come up with some smart reply to Melissa's insults, she always stumbled over her words and ended up looking even more stupid than before. She was scared of Melissa, and Melissa knew it – that was the trouble.

'It's a pity Jamie Underhill's left,' Caz said. 'He'd have been sitting in between you if he was still here, wouldn't he? Mind you, I think I'd sooner have Melissa. At least she doesn't fiddle with a Game Boy the whole time.'

'Is it worth asking Mr Maclaren if you can move?' Sunny suggested.

Lauren shook her head. 'He says we have to stay in these places till half term. Then he'll have got to know us better, and he can work out where he wants us to sit.'

'Well then, you only have to put up with Melissa for a few more weeks,' Caz said reassuringly.

But Melissa could make a few weeks seem like an eternity, Lauren thought gloomily to herself as the bell rang for the end of break. How was she going to last that long?

That Saturday, Lauren invited her friends round to cook DIY pizzas. Her mum had made a big batch of dough and put out bowls of tomato sauce, grated cheese, sliced mushrooms and peppers, sweetcorn, olives and salami (though Lauren steered clear of that, being a vegetarian), so everyone could assemble their own.

'There! Mine's ready for the oven,' Caz said, dusting off her hands and standing back to admire the funny face she'd made with salami, mushrooms and olives.

'Just wait five minutes till Michelle's and Sunny's are done,' Lauren's mum Valerie told her, looking through the see-through oven door. 'Would you like some more lemonade in the meantime, honey?' Even though she'd lived in the UK for years, Valerie Turner hadn't lost her American accent. Lauren loved the way she sounded so different.

'Mine's ready too, Mum,' she said, adding a couple more sweetcorn teeth between her pizza monster's red pepper lips.

Caz and Jess had been moaning on about the footie practice they'd had that morning. Mr Fielding, the games teacher who helped run the girls' team, had made them practise tackling the whole time and someone had kicked Jess on the shin.

'Why don't you give up?' Michelle asked, as she and Sunny tucked into their pizzas at the kitchen table. 'It's not like school, is it? You don't *have* to do it if it's no fun.' She flicked back her long brown hair and added, 'And if you're not that good at football, there probably isn't much point, is there? I mean, it's not like me going to drama class.'

Michelle was convinced she was going to be spotted by some talent scout sooner or later who would launch her on a glittering career in fashion or showbiz. She was tall, she had a great singing voice and she loved performing – or showing off, as Lauren sometimes thought. She would never have said that out loud, though; they were friends, after all.

Caz and Jess exchanged looks, as if trying to guess what the other was thinking. 'The trouble is . . .' Jess began, and then her voice tailed lamely away.

'. . . we promised Nikki we'd carry on,' Caz finished for her. 'She'll go spare if she comes back from America and finds out the team's fallen apart!'

'But she might not be back for a year,' Sunny said through a mouthful of cheese and tomato. 'Can you keep going that long? Through the winter and everything?'

'I don't know,' Jess muttered. 'The whole thing was a laugh when we started, but it's got so serious now. Mr Fielding's always going on at us about something or other.'

'Hey, that reminds me!' Caz said suddenly, fumbling for something in the pocket of her combats. 'How could I have forgotten? I got an e-mail from Nikki this morning, replying to that one we sent her on Thursday.'

She fished out a piece of paper, and the others immediately crowded around to read the latest instalment of news from California.

Yo, you guys!
Thanks for your message. Isn't e-mail great? It's so quick! Good to hear all your news. Wish I'd seen Melissa throwing Kimberley's bag over the wall! And Mr Mac sending her to the Head. There's a trouble-maker here, too - somebody keeps taking things from people's lockers and coat pockets. Sounds crazy, but I can't help wondering if it's Nancy. You know, the girl who looks like Melissa? Maybe she's a Melissa clone, ha ha!!!

I've got to know Lisa and Belle better, tho I'm not sure if we're going to be best friends. Anyway, they've invited me round at Hallowe'en. Apparently it's going to be a slumber party, so everyone's coming in their PJs and nighties.

LAUREN'S SPOOKY SLEEPOVER

Doesn't sound exactly spooktacular, does it? I'll let you know how it goes.

Hallowe'en is a really big deal here. People dress up to go trick-or-treating, and the houses are all decorated like haunted mansions. Belle showed me some photos of her party last year. It looked amazing! Her mum ('mom' is how they write it in the US) made a fake graveyard in the front yard (see, I'm turning American already!). Cardboard gravestones with funny things written on them and boots half-buried at one end, like someone was coming up out of the earth. Also they had dried flowers sprayed black and cobwebs everywhere in the house – with a skeleton sitting on the loo and a dry-ice machine so the place looked all misty. (A bit OTT, if you ask me.)

Gotta go now – time for footie practice. I'm glad the team's doing OK, Caz. You can

```
tell Mr Fielding I've made my first
touchdown. American football is wicked!

Missing you lots -
Nikki

PS - How are Frankie and Fred? Jess, I need
to know!
```

'Sounds like she's settling in,' Sunny said when she'd finished reading the note.

'And maybe if she gets really into American football, she won't mind if we don't carry on with the English version,' Caz added hopefully.

'I think we should give it up if we want to,' Jess decided. 'Sunny's right – Nikki can't expect us to carry on with something we're not enjoying for months and months. After all, I am looking after the rats for her, aren't I? I'll let her know how well they are and then she'll be so grateful—'

But she was interrupted by Lauren, who'd been reading the message through again. 'Oh, enough about your football club!' she said, with a glint in her eye. 'I've just had an idea! Why

18

don't *we* have a Hallowe'en party too? We can all dress up and make those freaky decorations Nikki was talking about. It'll be great!'

'As that does happen to be quite a good idea,' Jess told her, 'I will stop talking about footie – for now.'

'It's a brilliant idea!' Caz said enthusiastically. 'I think we all need cheering up.'

'And we haven't had a party for ages,' Sunny added. 'Not since Nikki left, anyway.'

'So that's settled,' Michelle said, licking her fingers as she finished her pizza. 'A Hallowe'en party it is. And let's make the place look *really* scary!'

'Hmm. Maybe,' Lauren said doubtfully. She wasn't quite so sure about that . . .

'Now, look. I'm happy for you girls to throw a Hallowe'en party here, but there have to be a few rules,' Lauren's mum said firmly, drying her wet hands on a tea towel as she finished washing up after lunch. 'We can't end up with gangs of kids roaming round the neighbourhood in the dark and frightening everybody half to death. If you

19

go trick-or-treating, Dad or I come with you and we only call on people we know. Got that?'

'OK, Mum,' Lauren said. She wasn't keen on wandering around strange houses at night, anyway! There was no telling who you might meet.

'And as it'll be the half-term holiday, you can have a sleepover afterwards,' Mrs Turner went on. 'But you have to swear faithfully not to keep each other up all night with scary stories, just because it's Hallowe'en. Sunny, that means you – OK?'

'OK,' Sunny nodded, looking shamefaced. She was an amazing storyteller: too amazing, in fact. Lauren would never forget the sound of her soft voice in the darkness, going on and on about some poor girl who'd fallen down a lift shaft. That was the spine-chilling tale she'd come up with to entertain her friends on one of their last sleepovers. Lauren had had nightmares for weeks afterwards and she still shivered when she thought about the story, which she tried very hard never to do. Particularly the ending, when—

Quickly, she forced herself to concentrate on

what her mother was saying. '. . . there might be a few Hallowe'en things up in the loft, if you'd like to go up and take a look.'

'But we want to make new ones, Mum,' she protested. 'We don't want some crumpled old pieces of cardboard left over from years ago. It'll look really lame!'

'Well, why don't we see what these things are like, at least?' Caz said.

'Yeah, come on,' Michelle said, leading the way out of the kitchen. 'This has to be a real spookfest, right? The more decorations, the better!'

It was cold up in the loft, and dark. There was only one small window which overlooked the Turners' back garden. Jess made her way over to it, being careful not to hit her head on the loft's low cross beams, and rubbed on the grimy glass so she could see out.

'Hey, Caz! There's Michael,' she said, beckoning her over. 'Come over here!'

Down below, Caz's stepfather was hacking at some overgrown trees and bushes near a large shed at the end of their garden, to the left of Lauren's. This shed was Caz's hangout – she and her friends had decorated the place and they'd spent lots of time there in the summer.

'That part of the garden's a real jungle,' Caz said, craning to look through the window. 'Michael wants to clear it so we can sit out there next year. We might put a hammock up too.'

'That's a good idea,' Jess said. 'But, hey – look at the garden on the other side of Lauren's. Now that's what I call a jungle! Who lives there, Laurie?'

Lauren looked up from the box she and Michelle had just opened. 'Oh, this old lady called Mrs Cooper,' she said absent-mindedly. 'I've never seen her go into the garden, but her dog's always out there.'

'Oh, yes! I can see him,' Caz said, peering down. 'A little sandy-coloured one. Look – in the bushes, Jess. I love it up here! You can get a bird's-eye view of everything that's going on.'

'Hang on, I remember this!' Sunny broke in, unfolding a large sheet of paper and holding up the cut-out figure of a witch with a big bulbous nose. 'Didn't we use it for a game at one of your parties a couple of years ago, Lauren?'

'Yeah, that's right,' Lauren replied. 'Stick the gum on the witch's nose.' She took a closer look at the picture and said, 'She's still in quite good shape. We might have to patch up her nose a bit, but that shouldn't be too difficult. Why don't we take her downstairs and call it a day? I don't think there's much else up here.'

She wasn't about to admit it, but poking around in the loft was giving her the creeps. There was something sad about the piled-up boxes and bags, filled with things that nobody wanted any more. Musty books that would never be read, outgrown clothes that would probably end up in a charity shop, and toys that she'd loved once upon a time now looking dirty and forlorn.

'Last one down has to put up the loft ladder!' she said, heading towards it. Suddenly, she couldn't wait to get back to the light and warmth.

Mrs Turner was poring over a book spread out on the kitchen table, looking for Hallowe'en party ideas. 'There are all kinds of things we could make,' she said, looking up as they all trooped in. 'Pumpkin lanterns and spiders out of pipecleaners, and balloon ghosts. I'd better dig out some white lining material.'

Lauren's mum ran her own business from home, making soft furnishings: curtains, blinds, cushions and tablecloths. The spare room was full of fabric that she'd picked up here and there and was keeping in case it came in handy some day.

'Oh, yes,' Lauren said, coming to look over her mother's shoulder. 'Hey! There's a picture of some fake gravestones, just like the ones Nikki was talking about. They look amazing, don't they?'

'Sure they're not too frightening?' her mum said. 'We don't want to give anyone nightmares.'

'Oh, no one's going to worry about some old pieces of cardboard,' Jess said, with a flick of her auburn hair. 'Listen, would anyone mind if I went outside for a kick around? I've got

Matt's football with me and the sun's just come out.'

'Go ahead,' Lauren smiled. Jess was usually the first to get bored with whatever it was they were doing, and looking through a book for party ideas obviously didn't appeal to her right now.

'I'll come with you,' Caz said. 'If that's OK, Lauren? No headers though, Jess.'

'Don't worry,' Jess told her. 'This is strictly for fun – it's not a Fielding-style torture session!'

After the two of them had gone out to the garden, Lauren got down to business with Sunny and Michelle. Before long, they'd drawn up a list of the people they wanted to invite: Lauren had the casting vote, of course, because it was really her party. Mrs Turner had come up with some great scary games they could play and all kinds of spooky food to eat. They were in the middle of discussing freaky costumes when Jess came bursting back into the kitchen, with Caz close behind.

'Emergency!' she announced urgently. 'I've kicked Matt's ball over the fence. We'll have to go round and ask the old lady if we can get it back.'

'Rather you than me,' Lauren said. 'Mrs Cooper is a real dragon! She hates kids, doesn't she, Mum?'

'I'm afraid she does,' Mrs Turner said. 'The Wilsons' boy, two doors up, was always kicking his footballs over her fence and she lined them all up in the front window like they were trophies. Wouldn't give them back for ages.'

'Could *you* ask her for me then, Valerie?' Jess said. Her face had gone very white, so that her freckles stood out like vivid orange speckles. 'She's more likely to listen to you. Please – it's important!'

'I can try,' Mrs Turner said. 'But I wouldn't hold out much hope. She may not even answer the door.'

Jess paced up and down the kitchen while they waited for Lauren's mum to come back from Mrs Cooper's. 'Don't worry,' Lauren told her reassuringly. 'You'll probably get the ball back eventually.'

She couldn't understand why Jess seemed so

upset. It was only a football, wasn't it? Matt probably had loads more at home.

'Eventually isn't good enough,' Jess said miserably, flopping down into a chair at the table. 'You don't understand! That ball is Matt's most precious possession: it's been signed by the whole England team! Dad won it in a raffle and gave it to him for his last birthday. I only borrowed it to show off to Mr Fielding because Matt's out for the day. If he finds out I've laid so much as a finger on it, he'll go bananas!'

She buried her head in her hands, and they had to strain to hear her muffled voice. 'I *have* to get that football back, no matter what it takes – or my life won't be worth living!'

'Can you see it?' Lauren asked anxiously, hovering about at the edge of the flowerbed. Jess had one foot wedged in Caz's linked hands and was scrabbling for a toehold on the garden fence with the other.

Lauren's mum had come back from Mrs Cooper's with the bad news that the old lady wasn't answering her door, so Jess had decided it was time for direct action. A little thing like a two-metre fence with thorny rose bushes on either side wasn't going to put her off!

'Nearly there,' she replied, at last managing to haul herself up and peer over into Mrs Cooper's overgrown garden.

'Maybe *you* should have climbed up,' Sunny said to Michelle. 'You're the tallest, after all. You'd have had a better view.'

'No way!' Michelle was horrified. 'This skirt's much too tight! Besides, it's not my football and *I* didn't kick it over the fence. Goodness knows why Jess had to take it out here in the first place, if it's so precious,' she added in an undertone.

'I heard that!' Jess's flushed, indignant face turned round from her perch on the fence. 'It's all very well to say that now, isn't it? I made a mistake, all right? It sometimes happens – even to you, Miss Perfect.'

'Oh, stop squabbling!' Caz pleaded. 'Hurry up and look for the ball, Jess! This is really uncomfortable.'

'OK, OK.' Jess turned back and gazed over the fence again. 'Got it!' she exclaimed a few seconds later. 'Well, I can see it, at least. It's caught in the rose bush about halfway down.'

'Here, take this.' Sunny passed Jess a garden stake she'd found lying in the flowerbed. 'You might be able to hook it towards you.'

'Thanks!' Jess grunted, leaning forward as

far as she possibly could and threshing around in the spiky branches with the stake. She reached out with her other hand and cried, 'I can nearly touch it! Can you get me up any higher, Caz?'

By now, Caz was red in the face with exertion. 'I'll try,' she groaned, steadying herself for one supreme effort.

'Be careful!' Lauren said, biting her lip. She could see the fence swaying dangerously and Jess looked so precarious, bent over the top with her bottom in the air. What if the whole thing fell down? What if Mrs Cooper saw her? What if—?

Suddenly there was a volley of furious barking from the other side of the fence. Caught by surprise, Jess screamed and wobbled – just as Caz managed to hoist her leg a little farther upwards. With a last despairing cry, Jess lost her balance completely. The other four watched, frozen in horror, as she pitched over and tumbled headlong into Mrs Cooper's garden.

They stared at each other for a moment in appalled silence. Sunny was the first to speak. 'Jessie! Gingernut!' she shouted, rushing up to the fence and putting her ear against it. 'Are you OK?'

Caz took a step back and looked up at the top of the fence, as though Jess might suddenly bounce back and appear in mid-air. 'Jess! Speak to us!' she called. 'What's happened?'

'Poor Jess,' Michelle said, biting her lip. 'And the last thing I said to her was really mean, too. Now I may never have a chance to say sorry!'

'Oh, stop being such a drama queen!' Sunny snapped, turning round. 'She's not dead! We all know what a tough cookie she is – it'll take more than a tumble to finish her off.'

'Then why doesn't she talk to us?' Lauren said, crowding behind the others close to the fence and calling Jess's name again. All they could hear was Mrs Cooper's dog, still barking frantically. 'What if she's hurt herself badly? Broken her leg or something? We'd better go and tell Mum what's happened.'

'If only I hadn't hoisted her up just then!' Caz muttered. 'It must have looked like I tipped her over the fence on purpose!' She broke off suddenly and said suspiciously, 'You're not laughing, are you, Sunny?'

'No, of course I'm not!' Sunny replied, turning

her face away. 'But you've got to admit, that's exactly what it did look like.'

'Someone has to climb up and see what's happened,' Michelle said decisively. 'I'd volunteer but, like I said, I'm not exactly dressed for it. Caz, you're too heavy. It'll have to be Sunny or Lauren.'

'Wait!' The barking had suddenly stopped and Lauren held up her hand for silence. 'I heard something then! Jess? Is that you?'

A faint voice came floating over from the other garden towards them. 'I'm OK,' Jess was saying. 'I've got the ball.'

'Are you hurt?' Caz demanded, at the same time as Michelle asked, 'What's the dog doing? He's gone very quiet.'

'He's licking my face,' Jess answered. 'I think I'm all right. The fall winded me for a second, that's all.'

'How are you going to get back?' Sunny asked. 'Shall we reach over and pull you up?'

'No, don't do that,' came the reply. 'I'm too sore to go mountaineering.'

And then a sudden note of panic entered Jess's

voice. 'Oh, help! Mrs Cooper's coming! Quick, you lot – scatter!'

Her friends didn't need telling twice. They took one look at each other and rushed madly back to the safety of the house.

'If Jess isn't back in the next couple of minutes, I think we should go round there and get her out,' Sunny said, looking up at the kitchen clock.

At least ten minutes had passed and there was still no sign of her. Luckily, Lauren's mum was somewhere upstairs; they were all hoping Jess would reappear before she guessed what had happened.

'What *can* she be doing?' Lauren was nearly frantic with worry. 'Or rather, what's being done to her? Oh, why didn't we stay there to stick up for her instead of running away?'

'Come on, surely Mrs Cooper can't be as bad as that!' Caz said. 'The worst she can do is give Jess a good telling-off.'

'Why are you so scared of her, Laurie?' Michelle asked. 'Do you know something we don't?'

Lauren thought for a while. Mrs Cooper looked so grim, with her dark, deep-set eyes and thin lips that always seemed to be clamped tightly together, but that wasn't the only reason Lauren felt uncomfortable around her. Maybe it was the fact that the old lady lived all on her own, except for her dog. Lauren's home was always full of noise and activity. She didn't have any brothers or sisters, but she had friends round all the time and so did her parents – there was usually someone sitting in the kitchen having a cup of tea and a gossip.

Yet on the other side of the wall that joined their two semi-detached houses, Mrs Cooper led such a solitary life. Lauren sometimes heard the dog bark or a door slam, but that was about it. There were hardly any visitors, apart from Mrs Cooper's son who called every now and then. She certainly wasn't interested in friendly chats with her neighbours! Lauren's mum had been given the brush-off loads of times. Mrs Cooper didn't seem to need any human contact – that was what made her so spooky.

All that was hard to explain. 'She's like the witch in *Hansel and Gretel*,' Lauren settled for. 'You know, the one who lived in a gingerbread house and shoved those children in the oven?'

Caz shivered. 'Come on, let's go and see what's happening,' she said, jumping up. 'Though I still can't believe that poor old lady you're so mean about would hurt a fly.'

But when they flung open Lauren's front door – there was Jess, about to ring the bell. Large as life and perfectly all right, if still rather pale. Matt's football was tucked safely under one arm and a hairy, sandy-coloured dog was frisking around her heels on the end of a lead, looking very pleased with himself.

'Jess!' they shrieked, gathering round to give her a hug and talking all at once. 'Are you OK? Where have you been? What's been going on? And what are you doing with that dog?'

When Jess was safely installed in the kitchen – plus dog – she told them what had happened. 'Well, now I know what you mean about Mrs

Cooper being a dragon,' she began. 'I got a major telling-off for being in her garden!'

'Fair enough, I suppose,' Sunny put in. 'She hadn't exactly invited you round for tea, had she?'

'Maybe not,' Jess conceded. 'And I did make a mess of her rose bush. Anyway, she went on and on about how I'd disturbed her afternoon rest and how she wasn't at all well at the moment and the doctor had said she shouldn't be out in the cold—'

'Come to think of it, I haven't seen her about recently,' Lauren said thoughtfully. 'She usually takes her dog for a walk first thing, when we're going off to school.'

'You still haven't told us why you've got the dog,' Michelle said, giving the little terrier a pat. 'He's quite cute, isn't he? What's his name?'

'He's called Charlie,' Jess said, ruffling the dog's fur and getting a handful of licks in return. 'That was my master stroke! When I could get a word in edgeways, I offered to take him to the park for her. It was the only way I could see to get out of there! Mrs Creepy Cooper was threatening to call the police and complain to your parents, Laurie.'

Lauren winced. She didn't want anything getting in the way of her party plans, and a lecture from Mrs Cooper would almost certainly put paid to her chances of a sleepover. 'So what did she say about that?' she asked Jess.

'I think she was quite pleased, though she'd have died rather than admit it,' Jess replied. 'She said it would have to be a decent long walk to make up for all the trouble I'd caused and that I was to take very good care of Charlie. The only really disgusting part is that – wait for it – when he poops, we have to put our hand in a plastic bag and pick it up! Can you imagine? Gross!'

There were more shrieks and giggles at this. 'What do you mean, "we"?' Sunny asked, when they'd recovered themselves a little. 'That's your job, isn't it, Jess? After all, you were the one who kicked the ball over in the first place.'

'I might find it hard to bend down,' Jess said, pulling a face and holding her side. 'I think that fall's done something to my back.'

'Seriously, though – are you sure you're OK?'

Caz asked. 'You must have landed with a real thump.'

'Well, I kind of slithered down headfirst,' Jess grinned. 'There were some branches on the other side that broke my fall. Just as well I was wearing jeans and long sleeves.' She held out her hands, which were covered in scratches.

'Then perhaps we should get going,' Michelle said, standing up and smoothing down her skirt. 'Come on, Charlie. Walkies!'

'Shall we take this with us for a kickabout?' Sunny asked innocently, picking Matt's football up from the table and twirling it on the end of her fingers.

'Sunny!' Jess shrieked, grabbing the ball and holding it tightly against her chest. 'That is *so* not funny!'

4

The next week, Lauren's party preparations began in earnest. She often thought the pre-match
build-up was the best part – making the invitations and decorations, thinking about what to eat
and drink, deciding what to wear and fiddling
about with her hair for ages. That, and talking
everything over afterwards with her friends.

After some experimenting with pumpkins and
witches' hats, Lauren decided to go for haunted
house invites. Once all the party info was filled in
she drew some spiders' webs, bats and creepy
cats in gold ink as a finishing touch.

'There! What do you think, Mum?' she asked,
holding her first finished invite at arm's length
and looking at it critically.

'Fantastic!' Mrs Turner said, giving her a hug.

'That's really effective!'

'It is, isn't it?' Lauren sighed with satisfaction and started on the rest of the batch. There was nothing she liked better than dreaming up an arty idea and then seeing whether she could make it work. Sometimes it didn't, which was frustrating, but her failures could often be turned into something different.

Because Lauren wasn't asking that many girls from her class, she had to be discreet about giving out the party invitations. There was no problem with Michelle, Caz, Sunny and Jess, as she saw them all the time. She decided to try and catch the other guests after school, before she and Caz set off home together.

The only trouble was, Melissa was always hanging around by the gates, waiting for her older sister. She seemed to have an inbuilt radar system for picking up whatever anyone particularly *didn't* want her to know about. If you'd had a geeky haircut at the weekend, Melissa would be the first to spot it and tell everyone else. And if your mum was wearing something totally embarrassing when she collected you from school,

Melissa was bound to notice. She didn't miss a thing, and she liked nothing better than making other people feel uncomfortable and embarrassed. Lauren in particular, for some reason.

Sure enough, as soon as Lauren caught up with Leanne Fielding to hand over her invite after school on Wednesday, Melissa materialised out of nowhere.

'Oh, isn't that sweet?' she cooed, grabbing the invitation. Lauren had run out of envelopes so her haunted house was exposed to Melissa's withering gaze. Somehow it didn't look quite so cool now.

'Are all your little friends going to dress up and go twick or tweating?' Melissa went on in the same sugary tone. 'Better not stay up too late or your mummies will be cwoss.'

Leanne was great, though. 'I hope so,' she said, snatching the card out of Melissa's hand. 'Fancy dress parties are such a laugh! Thanks, Laurie – I'd love to come.'

Melissa looked furious. 'Wouldn't catch me making a fool of myself like that,' she snapped. 'My sister's inviting her mates over and we're going to watch scary videos all night. Bet *you've* never seen an 18!'

'I wouldn't want to,' Lauren said to Caz on the way home. 'I hate horror films, don't you?'

'Oh, don't pay any attention to Melissa,' Caz said, hitching up her schoolbag. 'She's probably jealous. Anyway, she wouldn't need to dress up – she could come as herself: a blood-sucking vampire.'

Lauren laughed and began to feel better. 'It's weird that there's a girl in Nikki's new school who looks just like her,' she said, dawdling along the pavement. 'Maybe there's a secret society with Melissa lookalikes all over the world . . .'

'Dedicated to being mean and horrible,' Caz went on, starting to giggle.

'With prizes for the nastiest insults,' Lauren added. 'And if you make anyone cry you get a special badge.' They were both soon killing themselves with laughter, just thinking about it.

Eventually Caz wiped her eyes. 'I wonder how Nikki is?' she said. 'I thought she'd have answered that e-mail we sent her on Saturday by now.'

After they'd come back from taking Charlie for a walk the previous weekend, the four of them had gone round to Caz's house and sent Nikki a long e-mail. They'd told her all about Jess falling into Mrs Cooper's garden, and how embarrassing it had been in the park. (Charlie had pooped right in front of a group of boys hanging around by the playground, and he'd cocked his leg everywhere – even against an old man sitting on a bench!) Lastly, Lauren had told Nikki about their plans for a Hallowe'en party.

'I was hoping she could give us some cool ideas for scary costumes,' Lauren said. 'D'you think she's OK?'

'She's probably just busy,' Caz said. 'Talking of costumes – have you decided what to wear?'

'Not yet,' Lauren replied, skirting round a lamppost. 'Mum and I have been concentrating on decorations. We're going to the shopping centre on Saturday to see what's around. D'you want to come?'

'Sure!' Caz said, her eyes lighting up. 'And I

bet the others would, too. Feels like we haven't been shopping for months!'

'Michelle!' Jess exclaimed in exasperation. 'If you don't stop humming I'm going to shove this serviette in your mouth!'

It was late Saturday morning and Michelle, Lauren, Caz and Jess were sitting in a café at the shopping centre with Lauren's mum, having something to eat and waiting for Sunny to arrive.

'Oh, sorry,' Michelle replied airily. 'But we're learning this new song at my drama class and it's really catchy. Listen!' She started singing in a loud voice and some people at the neighbouring tables turned around to stare. Michelle wasn't worried about that, of course – she loved an audience.

'Miche! Stop it,' Lauren hissed. 'Everyone's looking!'

'Now, settle down, guys,' Mrs Turner said, draining her coffee. 'Oh, good. Here's our food.'

'And here's Sunny,' Caz said, catching sight of her hurrying towards the café with her mum. 'Right on time.'

The café wasn't too crowded yet, so Mrs Kumar sat at a separate table with Lauren's mother. They were soon deep into a gossip session.

'Sorry we're late,' Sunny gasped breathlessly to her friends. 'Dad's taking Anisha swimming and we couldn't find her costume.' She slid into the bench seat and added, 'No one wants to adopt a ready-made little sister, do they? I could do with a break.'

She ordered a mango smoothie before the waitress disappeared, then turned to Lauren and said, 'Laurie, about the party – it's good news and bad news. The bad news is that we're having a big family get-together that night for Diwali. I'm really sorry! Mum's just told me.'

'Oh, no!' Lauren's face fell. She felt bad enough having a party without Nikki – if Sunny couldn't be there either, it would be a real shame.

'You know how important Diwali is. It's like the start of our New Year,' Sunny said apologetically. 'We're having fireworks and everything. But listen – here's the good news. Mum says I can come to the sleepover at your house afterwards.

Would that be OK? I could get to you by about nine.'

'Sure,' Lauren said, making an effort to be positive. 'That would be great!' There were going to be lots of people at the party – as long as Sunny made the sleepover it would be OK.

'And we'll still have loads of time to have fun,' Jess put in, starting on her bacon sarnie.

'Now I've got that out of the way, there's something else we need to talk about,' Sunny went on. There was a note in her voice which made the others sit up and pay attention: this sounded important.

'Here,' she said, laying a piece of paper in the middle of the table. 'It's a message from Nikki. It arrived on Thursday, but I only checked my e-mails this morning.'

'Lauren and I were wondering when she was going to get in touch,' Caz said. 'She never replied to that e-mail we sent her on Saturday.'

'I know,' Sunny said, taking a slurp of her smoothie which had just arrived. 'I e-mailed her on Wednesday and asked if everything was OK. Well, it's not. Read that!'

LAUREN'S SPOOKY SLEEPOVER

Dear Sunny,

Sorry I haven't got back to you sooner. It was really great to get your message and it sounds like you're having fun. I wish I was back with you, that's for sure!

Life's not going so well here. Remember I told you in my last e-mail that things have been going missing at our school? This is going to sound incredible, but rumours have started that — wait for it — the thief is me! *I'm* the one who's meant to have been taking stuff from people's pockets and lockers! I can hardly even bear to write this down, but I know you won't believe it. (I hope you don't!)

I feel really alone here, apart from Lisa and Belle. They're the only ones who are talking to me at the moment. They told me about the rumours in the first place. Apparently there wasn't any trouble before I came, which is why everyone has decided I must be the one who's stealing. My teacher hasn't said anything yet, but she keeps on looking at me and I can see exactly what she's thinking.

You can let the others read this. I know my real friends will always be there for me. Mum and Dad say I've got nothing to worry about, but how can I help it? Things are so bad at school.

E-mail soon and cheer me up!
Nikki XXXXX

'Oh, poor Nikki!' Lauren stared at the e-mail in disbelief. She didn't believe for one second that those rumours about Nikki being a thief were true. Nikki was as straight as a die; she'd never take so much as a stick of chewing gum from anyone without asking. But who would make up such horrible stories about her, and why? Maybe it was that Melissa clone, Nancy, causing trouble.

'We'll have to e-mail her as soon as we get home,' Caz said, frowning. 'And perhaps we could send her a present? A pair of earrings or something small like that.'

'Let's make a tape to cheer her up,' Michelle said. 'Can we use your dictaphone, Sunny?'

As a leaving present, Sunny had given Nikki one of those mini tape recorders her dad used in the office to dictate letters. The Kumars had one at home too, and the idea was that she and Nikki could send tapes back and forth to each other.

'Sure,' Sunny said, deep in thought as she re-read Nikki's message. She looked up and added, 'I bet Nikki's school has a website – most of them do in America. Why don't we e-mail the Head or someone and tell them how great Nikki is and how she's never stolen anything in her life?'

Jess wrinkled her nose. 'We don't know for sure how far these rumours have spread,' she replied doubtfully. 'What if they're just going round the class and none of the teachers have heard yet? It might make everything ten times worse.'

'I wish she wasn't so far away,' Lauren said, taking a bite of her cheese and tomato toastie. 'Hang on! Does anyone have her phone number? We could give her a ring, couldn't we?'

Nobody did have Nikki's number, so they decided to ask her for it in the next e-mail and then ring from Lauren's house. 'Do you know what the time difference is in California?' Jess asked Sunny. (That was exactly the kind of thing she *would* know.)

'I think they're about eight hours behind us,' Sunny replied. 'We'd have to ring in the evening, or the weekend when she's not at school.'

Lauren looked up at the clock on the café wall. So now it would be half past four in the morning where Nikki was. She tried to picture her, all alone in that great big bedroom with the walk-in closet, and put down her half-eaten sandwich, suddenly losing her appetite. Poor Niks, she must be feeling so miserable! Maybe she couldn't sleep, or was having nightmares – Lauren certainly would be, in her shoes! Her own problems with Melissa didn't seem half so important now, compared to what Nikki was facing.

'Well, I don't think there's anything else we can do now,' Sunny sighed. 'Are we about ready to hit the shops?'

'I am,' Michelle said, finishing the last of her chips. 'I've had this great idea for my costume! There are one or two things I need to add the finishing touch.'

'Like what?' Jess said. 'Oh, come on, Miche – let us in on the secret! I haven't got a clue what to wear.'

But Michelle wouldn't give anything away, no matter how much they threatened to tickle and tease her or give her really outrageous dares on the Hallowe'en sleepover. Lauren managed to cheer up a little, but there was no way she was going to forget about Nikki. She'd make her a special card as soon as they got home . . .

The next week at school seemed to last for ever, like the week before a holiday always does. Lauren couldn't wait for half term! She'd have a break from Melissa, for one thing, and then with a bit of luck she'd be sitting next to someone else when they came back to school. Her Hallowe'en party would be on the Monday and after that she'd have loads of time to hang out with her friends. Michelle was going to stay with her gran for a couple of days near the end of the week, but Sunny, Jess and Caz were around the whole time.

The weather was turning colder. Fog

shrouded the trees one morning as Lauren and Caz shuffled through damp leaves on their way to school, and their breath hung mistily on the air in front of them.

'Winter's on its way,' Lauren's mum said with a shiver that evening, drawing the thick living-room curtains. 'Let's make a fire.'

She switched on a couple of lamps, casting golden pools of light over the polished wooden tables. Lauren snuggled deeper into the sofa cushions. She much preferred the summer sunshine, but there *was* something cosy about being snug indoors while the wind howled outside.

'By the way, Laurie,' her mother said, piling coals into the fireplace with a pair of tongs, 'I saw Mrs Cooper today. She asked if you girls could give Charlie another walk at the weekend, and I said you'd be glad to. Perhaps you could take him out a couple of times over half term, too?'

'Oh, Mum!' Lauren protested. 'Do I have to? It's so cold and horrible out there!'

'Well, wrap up warm then,' Mrs Turner replied, striking a match. 'You can spare half an hour of your time, can't you? Please, Lauren!

You'd be doing Mrs Cooper a big favour. She really doesn't look very well at all.'

'I bet she won't thank me for it,' Lauren muttered. When they'd brought Charlie home after that last walk, Mrs Cooper had hustled him inside and practically slammed the door in their faces!

'You'll get your reward in heaven,' her mum said, sitting back on her heels and patting Lauren's knee. 'Offer it up to the Lord, as my granny used to say.'

'Oh, all right then,' Lauren yawned, stretching her arms. After all, Charlie was a cute dog and it was great having him around. He had a shaggy, honey-coloured coat and a pinky-grey nose: it looked like it had once been painted black, but now the paint was wearing off and pink was showing through. He wagged his tail the whole time and, best of all, he didn't seem to make her wheeze. She'd always wanted to have a pet, but her mum was worried that animal hair might make her asthma worse. Perhaps the doctor was right and she really was growing out of it.

54

'Good girl,' Mrs Turner smiled. 'I know Mrs Cooper's not exactly the friendliest person in the world, but I don't think she means to be rude. She's probably just shy.'

'Huh!' Lauren snorted. That was a convenient excuse. She was shy herself, but she'd never get away with being as grumpy as Mrs Cooper. Changing the subject, she asked, 'Can we start making the piñata tonight, Mum? We need to get a move on if it's going to be ready for painting by the weekend.'

Piñatas were great for parties. They were a traditional Mexican festival treat, big round clay pots filled with little gifts and hung from the ceiling. People wore blindfolds and tried to hit the piñata with a stick, hoping it would shatter and all the tiny presents inside would fall into their hands. Lauren made her piñatas out of papier-mâché, which was easier to break and less mess to clear up! And for this party, she'd decided to decorate it like a pumpkin, with orange and black crêpe paper streamers.

I wonder if Nikki's going to be having a piñata at her party, Lauren thought to herself as she began tearing newspaper into strips. San Diego was near the border with Mexico – Nikki had told them that – so she probably would be. That's if she was still invited to the party, of course. Perhaps Lisa and Belle would have changed their minds and told her not to come.

While they stuck newspaper strips on to a balloon with wallpaper paste to make the piñata, Lauren told her mum about Nikki's last e-mail.

'Don't worry,' Mrs Turner said comfortingly. 'I'm sure it'll turn out to be a storm in a teacup. Nikki's parents are right – if she hasn't taken anything, she's got no reason to worry.'

'You don't think she *has* been stealing, do you?' Lauren was outraged that her mother could even hint at the idea. 'You know Nikki's not like that!'

'Sure, but sometimes people do strange things when they're unhappy,' Mrs Turner said, positioning a slippery strip of paper carefully on the balloon. 'This must be a difficult time for Nikki. She's miles away from home and she's left all her friends behind. She might act out of character as a way of telling everyone she's feeling miserable, and we shouldn't be too hard on her if that's the case.'

'I bet you a million pounds it's not,' Lauren said stubbornly. She wiped her sticky hands on a damp cloth and added, 'Besides, why would Nikki tell us about it if she *has* been nicking things? Wouldn't she just keep quiet?'

'Well, maybe she thinks she's about to be rumbled and she wants to tell you her story first,' Mrs Turner replied. 'Oh, Laurie – don't get upset! I'm sure you're right and there's no truth in these rumours. It might be best to keep an open mind, that's all.'

However this turns out, we have to stick by Nikki, Lauren thought to herself. If only we could talk to her! E-mailing was loads better than writing a letter, but it still wasn't the same as hearing someone's voice. She looked at the half-finished piñata and sighed. It was hard to get fired up about a party when one of her friends was in trouble.

Suddenly a long peal on their doorbell disturbed the peaceful room. Caz was on the doorstep, all muffled up in her favourite stripy polo neck. One look at her face told Lauren she had something important to say.

'What's up?' she asked, taking her through to the kitchen.

'I've just checked my e-mails,' Caz replied breathlessly, waving another sheet of paper. 'This came from Nikki overnight. You'll never guess what's happened! It's completely unbelievable!'

'Hey! I can't see!' Michelle said, peering over Jess's shoulder. 'Hold it up a bit, will you?'

Caz had brought Nikki's e-mail into school first thing the next morning to show the others. Now they were all crowding round in the playground to try and read it before the bell went.

Caz was still hopping up and down with excitement. 'You won't believe this!' she said, hugging herself. 'My eyes nearly popped out of my head when I saw it last night!'

'Here, why don't you read it out to us?' Sunny said, passing the e-mail back to Caz. 'The bell's about to go and we'll never find out what's happened otherwise.'

Lauren had read Nikki's message at least five times the night before, so she wasn't quite as desperate as everyone else to hear what Caz was about to say. She glanced towards the school gates and noticed Melissa Wilkins arriving, tagging along behind a couple of girls in the local secondary school uniform, Lauren recognised the stripy silver tie. One of them had the same pinched face and sharp pointy nose as Melissa. That must be her sister, Lauren thought to herself, remembering what Melissa had said about them watching scary videos together at Hallowe'en. She looked mean!

Melissa walked along with her head down, ignored by the two older girls. When she came to the school gates, she glanced up ahead and called out hopefully, 'Bye! See you later!'

There was no reply; the girls ahead didn't even bother to look round, though they must have heard. Melissa pushed open the gates, flushing. Lauren quickly turned back to her friends. She would never have believed it, but she actually felt sorry for Melissa Wilkins. It was obvious that her sister couldn't be bothered with her.

'Now, this is the main bit,' Caz was saying. 'Oh, where was I again?'

'Hurry up!' Jess shrieked. 'The bell's going to ring any minute and I'll go mad if we don't find out soon!'

'OK, OK,' Caz said. 'Yeah, here we are.' And she started to read.

'I've been so wrong about everything! It's hard to know where to begin, but basically, Lisa and Belle (do you remember, the girls who sit next to me in class, who I thought were quite nice?) — they're the ones who were behind everything! And Nancy (the girl who looks like Melissa, tho that's not her fault) — she stuck up for me!

'The first thing that happened was Nancy told me that Lisa and Belle's Hallowe'en party wasn't a slumber party after all. She said everyone else was going in proper costumes and that they were all going to laugh at me when I turned up in my PJs.'

'Can you believe it?' Caz broke off to say. 'How horrible is that?'

'Don't talk – just read!' Michelle told her. 'Unless you want to get lynched?'

'Well, at first I didn't know whether to believe her or not,' Caz went on hastily. 'I still thought Lisa and Belle were my friends. Wrong!!!!! The next day, I opened my locker and found this purse inside that didn't belong to me. Lisa was with me and as soon as she saw it, she started shouting that I'd stolen her wallet and how could I do something like that when she'd trusted me and tried so hard to be my friend.'

'If I could get my hands on that girl . . . !' Sunny muttered, before Jess and Michelle shushed her.

'Of course, I remembered that when I'd last used my locker, Belle had been standing right next to me,' Caz read. 'She must have planted Lisa's wallet in there before I shut the door. But who would believe that? It was their word against mine. I had to go and see the Principal and I thought I'd die, it was so awful.'

Then just at that crucial moment, the bell went.

'You can't leave it there!' Jess hissed. 'Quickly, tell us the rest! Pretend you haven't heard the bell!'

'But the next day,' Caz gabbled, doing her best to oblige, 'Nancy overheard Lisa and Belle laughing about what they'd done on the school bus, and she told our teacher. Mrs Meredith (that's her name) called them in separately — and they fessed up! They each tried to blame the other one, but who cares whose idea it was? They're as horrible as each other! Nancy says they were jealous cos everyone was making such a fuss of me when I arrived. And Belle used to be the big

```
football star but I'm better than she is,
ha ha.'
```

At that point, Caz really had to stop – she was getting glared at by Mrs Pearce, the ogre who doubled up as a classroom assistant in her spare time. 'You can read the rest at break,' she whispered, sticking the e-mail back in her pocket. 'It's good news, though, isn't it?'

You can say that again, Lauren thought happily to herself as she stood in line. Nikki's problems seemed to be working out, it was the last day of school before the half-term holiday, and there was a party on the horizon. Things were definitely looking up!

'I know you're all excited about half term,' Mr Maclaren told the class when they'd come back from assembly for their first lesson. 'So I thought we'd do something different in English today.' He paused, to make sure everyone was looking at him. 'Listen carefully, because I'm only going to explain this once, and save any questions till the end. OK?' Everyone nodded.

'Right,' Mr Maclaren went on, waving a sandwich box in the air. 'Now I've written the name of every person in the class on a separate piece of paper, folded it up and put it in this box. You'll each take it in turns to draw out a paper, and I want you to write a paragraph in your books about the person you've chosen – *without* mentioning their name. Got that?'

Everyone nodded again – except for Hugh Morgan, who'd already lost interest and was picking his nose.

'And this is the most important part.' Mr Maclaren lowered his voice, to signal that something exciting was coming up. Melissa sat back and yawned to show *she* couldn't care less.

'You have to write at least three *positive* things about this person,' Mr Maclaren continued, his eyes gleaming enthusiastically. 'Three good points that the boy or girl you pick possesses. He or she might be excellent at football, for example, or kind to other people, or tidy and organised. And if you can think of more than three good points, just put them down – the more the merrier! When everyone's finished, I'll read out your pieces one by one and we'll see if we can all guess who the person is. Now, does everyone understand what they have to do?'

Becky Smith's arm shot up. 'What happens if you pick out your own name?' she asked.

'Good question!' Mr Maclaren smiled. 'Just fold the paper up again, put it back in the box and pick another.'

'What happens if you can't think of anything good about the person you've chosen?' Alex Coombes called out.

'Put up your hand if you have something to say please, Alex,' Mr Maclaren said sternly. 'And you'll just have to think a little harder, won't you? Everyone has some positive qualities – it's simply a question of looking for them.'

Then he went rather red and added, carefully avoiding looking at anyone in particular, 'I've noticed that some people in this class are very good at picking on others. Let's see if they can praise them, too.'

'This idea sucks!' Melissa snorted under her breath, folding her arms. But she reluctantly took a piece of paper when Mr Maclaren was standing in front of her with his sandwich box, glaring.

It was Lauren's turn next. Please don't let me end up with someone like Hugh – or Matt, she thought to herself, sifting through the rustling squares of paper. That could be soooo embarrassing! Jess would be bound to think Lauren fancied her brother if she said anything nice about him.

The reality was far worse. Lauren unfolded the scrap of paper she'd eventually chosen and stared at the name written on it.

She sat there, stunned. Of all the names she could have chosen, she had to pick that one! She couldn't find *one* good thing to say about Melissa – let alone three! She was a bully, who only ever seemed happy when she was making other people miserable.

But then the image of Melissa trailing disconsolately along behind her sister that morning flashed into Lauren's mind and she felt a twinge of guilt. Maybe Melissa didn't have anyone at home telling her how great she was, like Lauren's parents did all the time. She certainly didn't get much praise at school, that was for sure. Maybe no one *ever* said anything nice about her! This might be the first time in her life anyone had paid her a compliment, and Lauren was just going to have to get on with it and think one up. Plus two more for good measure.

I'll try and turn Melissa's bad points into good ones, she decided eventually. She picked up her pencil, propped her head on her left arm so Melissa couldn't see her work, and started to write . . .

After what only seemed like a few minutes, Mr Maclaren told everyone to stop writing and began collecting up the books. Lauren listened in a daze to the first few passages he read out. She knew Melissa would soon realise who had picked her name. Although Mr Mac did his best to hide the book covers so no one knew who had written what, Lauren's handwriting was swirlier than anyone else's and stood out a mile. What would Melissa think about her description?

She'd either decide Lauren was even more of a creep than she'd thought, or she'd beat her up for not being nice enough. It was a no-win situation.

'A jolly good effort,' Mr Maclaren said encouragingly, after they'd finally guessed that Tom Patterson was the person being described in the piece he'd just read. 'Having big feet might not usually be seen as a positive quality, but the writer has captured something of the essential Tom. Well done!'

Then came the moment Lauren had been dreading. Mr Mac picked up her book and started to read.

In some ways, I wish I was more like this person. She always knows what to say and is never lost for words. Also she knows what is cool and what isn't. If she wears a particular pair of shoes, everyone thinks those are the shoes they should wear as well. She is small and neat. Also she has beautiful shiny hair which always looks tidy.

It didn't take long for somebody to come up with Melissa's name. There were only a few girls in the class everybody thought of as cool, and none of the others was particularly small.

'An excellent description!' Mr Mac beamed. 'Exactly the kind of thing I had in mind, and very sensitively written. Ten out of ten!'

Lauren couldn't resist snatching a quick side-long glance at Melissa. She was sitting at the table with her arms folded again, and it was hard to tell exactly what she was thinking. If anything, she looked slightly surprised.

When the bell went for break at the end of the lesson, she turned to Lauren and said, 'It was you who wrote that bit about me, wasn't it?'

'Yes, it was,' Lauren replied, wondering what was coming next. She actually felt quite proud of herself for coming up with the only nice things anyone could possibly have said about Melissa without lying. But what would Melissa think?

It turned out that Melissa approved. 'I like what you said about my hair,' she said, swishing back her long, thick plait with a satisfied look.

'Oh, great,' Lauren said cautiously.

'You could do a lot more with yours, you know,' Melissa went on, eyeing Lauren's wild curls. 'Serum, that's what you need. You put it on when your hair's wet and it'll go into ringlets. Stops it looking frizzy.'

'Sure,' Lauren said, taken aback. 'Serum – I'll remember that.'

'There's this brilliant stall in the market where I get all my shampoo and conditioners,' Melissa told her. 'It's dead cheap. Give me the money after half term and I'll get some for you, if you like.'

And with that, she strolled out of the classroom before Lauren had time to stammer her thanks. There was no way she could ever imagine being friends with Melissa, but it was a big relief not to have her as an enemy for a change. She caught Mr Mac's eye as he tidied up the books and returned his smile with a beaming grin of her own.

'Wow! Your house looks amazing!' Michelle breathed, her eyes wide as she gazed around. 'How long did it take you to do all this?'

It was early on Monday evening – the last day of October, All Hallows' Eve, the night witches and spirits are meant to roam the earth! – and Jess and Michelle had just arrived at Lauren's house. They'd decided it would be much more fun if they all got dressed up together; Caz was due any minute.

'We made the pumpkin lanterns and stuff over the weekend,' Lauren replied, jigging from one foot to another with excitement. 'And Caz came round this afternoon to give us a hand.'

She was really pleased with the way every-thing had turned out. Downstairs, the house was dark and shadowy, with bats hanging down from the ceiling and furry spiders over the doorways which brushed against your face when you went through. Pumpkin lanterns with eerie, cackling faces were dotted everywhere – including outside on the porch to welcome the party guests. At the top of the stairs stood a terrifying witch, her cloak flying out behind and a broomstick in her hand. (That was a dressmaker's dummy, dressed in black with a hat and a fluorescent mask balanced on top. They'd even strapped a torch under the mask, to give her face a ghostly glow.)

Suddenly another dark shape made them all jump. 'Hi, girls!' said Lauren's dad, Daniel, emerging from the living room. He'd come home early that afternoon to help decorate the house. 'What do you think of my spooky sound effects CD?'

A cacophony of shrieks, groans, creaking doors and spine-chilling violin music drifted out of the room behind him.

'Brilliant!' Lauren grinned. That was the perfect finishing touch.

'Your dad's such a laugh,' Jess said as they thundered upstairs to Lauren's bedroom to start getting ready. 'I wish mine was a bit more like him.'

'Do you want to swap?' Lauren replied, remembering all the times her father had teased her or played some awful practical joke that had made her want to fall through the floor. She didn't really mean it, of course – Jess's dad was on the dull side, to be honest – but hers did tend to go over the top. He was planning a surprise for the party: she'd caught him chuckling about it but he'd refused to give her any clues, no matter how much she pleaded.

'Just don't embarrass me in front of my friends – please, Dad!' she'd begged.

'As if I'd do a thing like that!' he'd answered, pretending to look hurt. Lauren was not reassured.

'So come on, Michelle – out with it!' Jess demanded when they were up in Lauren's bedroom. 'What's this great costume of yours?'

'You won't be able to see it properly until I'm

all ready,' Michelle said, taking a black T-shirt and what looked like some leggings out of her carrier bag. 'But this should give you a clue!' And she held up a shape cut out of white sticky-backed plastic.

'It's a bone, isn't it?' Lauren said, taking a closer look. 'Oh I know! You're going to be a skeleton!'

'Dead right!' Michelle said, pulling on the black T-shirt. As her head popped out at the top, she exclaimed in surprise, 'Hey, I made a joke! *Dead* right! Get it?'

'Ha ha, very funny,' Lauren said. 'You should team up with Dad – that's about his level.'

Michelle didn't care. 'I've got this wicked skeleton mask to wear,' she went on, pulling it out of her carrier bag. 'And the costume looks amazing when all the bones are stuck on – we had a trial run at home. D'you think your mum could give me a hand, Laurie?'

'Here I am, ready to help,' Mrs Turner said, appearing in the doorway right on cue. 'And I found this creepy old woman lurking around on the doorstep, so I've invited her in too.'

They could see the tall point of a witch's hat behind her, with a hank of long black hair hanging down beneath it.

'Caz!' Jess shrieked. 'You're already dressed up. Cheater!'

'I couldn't resist it,' Caz grinned, taking off her hat and witchy wig. 'I haven't got any make-up on yet, though. Natalie's lent me some black lipstick and I've got green face paint for my cheeks. What do you think?'

(Natalie was Caz's stepsister. She was into the Gothic look and had a huge collection of black clothes and weird make-up – perfect for Hallowe'en!)

'Ace!' Lauren said, giving her a hug. 'And I love that plastic snake round your neck.'

'Whatever's that?' Michelle asked, pausing from assembling her skeleton to stare curiously at the black, hairy thing Jess had just taken out of her bag.

'This – ' Jess answered proudly, twirling it in the air, '– is my wig! Great, isn't it?'

'It's bit of a funny shape,' Michelle said doubtfully. 'Is it meant to be square?'

'Absolutely,' Jess told her, jamming on the wig and turning around. 'Guess who I am!'

'Frankenstein!' they all shouted at the same time, and Jess beamed delightedly.

'So the only person we don't know about is you, Laurie,' Caz said as she sat down in front of the mirror to make herself look properly witchy. 'What are you dressing up as?'

'I'll tell you when I get back from the loo,' Lauren replied, heading out of the door. Once her costume was on, it was difficult to sit down – let alone do anything else!

Half an hour later, they were all ready. Caz was a truly terrifying witch with spooky black lips and a wart on her nose, Michelle was an elegant but creepy skeleton, Jess was an out-of-this-world Frankenstein with bolts sticking out of her neck and a square head – and Lauren was a ghoulish mummy, fresh from the tombs of ancient Egypt . . .

She and her mum had torn an old sheet into strips and soaked them in tea so they looked old. Lauren put on a white T-shirt and tights and then her mum wound the strips around her legs, arms and body, keeping them in place with safety pins. She finished off with a bandage wound loosely round Lauren's head, criss-crossing her white-painted face a couple of times.

'OK, time for a photo shoot,' Mrs Turner said, grabbing her camera. 'Say cheese. No, say freak!'

'Let's go outside and wait for people to arrive!' Jess said after a couple of shots, so they piled downstairs and out of the front door.

Our costumes look even more scary in the dark, Lauren thought to herself, leaning against the doorway and watching her friends fool around in the street. That damp fog had appeared again, making everything seem hazy and unreal. She shivered – and then bit back a scream! Someone had propped an old dummy on a kitchen chair in their porch. Straw stuck out of the end of its sleeves and, beneath one of her father's old hats, a monster mask leered out at her. It looked terrifying! For one moment, Lauren actually thought it was real.

'That scarecrow's freaky!' Jess yelled. Lauren nodded and waved back, glad no one had spotted her about to make a fool of herself. She put one hand over her thumping heart and gave the dummy's Wellington boot a little kick, to pay it back for giving her such a fright.

A car was drawing up outside their house. Jess, Caz and Michelle gathered around it, letting out their best spooky cackles and groans. Amid lots of giggling, a zombie and another witch climbed out – Kimberley and Leanne.

'Welcome!' Lauren boomed in a deep voice, holding her arms out in front of her as she walked down towards them, keeping her legs stiff and mummy-like. 'We've been expecting you for years. Thousands of years!'

'This is so cool!' Leanne cried, waving her long plastic fingernails as she led the way back up to the house, with Lauren and the others close behind. 'Doesn't everyone look amazing?'

And then suddenly, they all got the fright of their lives. Leanne had one foot poised on the top step when she let out the most bloodcurdling, ear-piercing scream Lauren had ever heard. Not

that she had any time to think
about it – she was screaming, too.

With one terrifying, jerky move-
ment, the scarecrow had jumped off
the chair and was standing in front of them. Its
long dangly arms flapped to and fro, barring
their way into the house, and its ghoulish head
was lolling crazily to one side.

They were all screaming fit to burst. Lauren
couldn't move – she was frozen to the spot in
panic, her eyes fixed on the apparition in front of
her. Dimly, she became aware of someone push-
ing past her. 'No! Stop!' she shrieked, unable to
believe her eyes as Jess marched up to the monster and stretched one arm towards its grinning
face . . .

'Dad! I'm going to kill you!' Lauren screeched
when she'd got her breath back. 'And don't think
I don't mean it, because I do!'

Half an hour later, Lauren's house was full of ghosts (Emma, Nasreen and Roxanne in white sheets with painted white faces and flour in their hair), vampires (Sophie and Louise with cloaks, plastic teeth and loads of fake blood), witches (Caz, Kelly and Leanne, all in black, with pointed hats and broomsticks), zombies (Sarah and Kimberley with white faces, black-ringed eyes and green hair) and a garbage monster (Dionne, dressed in a plastic dustbin bag with litter and rubbish taped all over it and a necklace of empty cans strung around her neck). Plus a skeleton, Frankenstein, and a fast-disintegrating mummy, of course.

They rushed through the house, shrieking and giggling at the scary decorations. The big hit of the evening was the fake graveyard that Lauren and her mum had set up in the back garden. The cardboard tombstones looked great, looming out of the darkness, and the rhymes on them were so silly that no one could possibly be frightened. 'Here I lie, for ever more. Bend down close, you'll hear me snore,' read one, and another: 'Here lies Nelly, ten foot deep. She always liked her beauty sleep.'

'I don't get this,' Caz said, standing over a tilted tombstone and staring at the inscription.

'It's my dad's tragic sense of humour,' Lauren explained apologetically. 'Say it out loud and then you'll understand.'

'Here lies the sad victim of a clifftop accident: Eileen Dover,' Caz read, and then giggled. 'That's quite funny, actually.'

After they'd floated and zoomed and marched around the graveyard, posing for more pictures, they split up into two groups to go trick-or-treating. Lauren's mum had checked out the neighbours first, so she knew which houses it would be OK to call at. First on the list was Caz's. The front door creaked slowly open, and there were more bloodcurdling shrieks as her step-sister Natalie jumped out from behind it to give everyone a scare.

'Have some treats, my dears,' she cackled, holding out a carrier bag – and then burst out laughing as their fingers touched a horrible slimy mess at the bottom.

'Yuck!' Michelle exclaimed, snatching back her hand as though it had been burnt. 'What *is* that?'

'Cold spaghetti and mayonnaise,' Natalie replied. 'I thought you'd like it.'

Back home, they played a couple of rounds of Murder in the Dark and then it was time to eat all the spooky food laid out on a table littered with spiders and cobwebby dried flowers, sprayed black. There was spaghetti in tomato sauce to look like guts, crispy potato skins – witches' fingernails – with a green avocado swamp dip, and spiders made out of crackers sandwiched together with cheese spread and Twiglets for legs. And for the meat eaters, there were mini–frankfurters dipped in tomato sauce and arranged on cocktail sticks to look like bloody fingers (gross!). To drink, there was a big bowl of punch with frozen 'hands' floating in it (clear plastic gloves filled with juice) and a plastic snake coiled menacingly over the edge.

When they'd finished eating, Lauren's dad told them to come through to the living room for some more ghostly entertainment. They arranged themselves, giggling nervously, in a circle on the floor. Mr Turner was still wearing his scarecrow costume and he really did look scary as he took his seat in a shrouded armchair. With a sudden snap that made them jump, he switched off the one dim lamp and plunged the room into total darkness. Scary music played softly in the background as he began to speak in a low, ghostly voice.

'Did I ever tell you about the house I had to work on last year?' he began. (Lauren's dad ran a building company, so the story made sense – so far.) 'Well, me and a few of the lads were doing up this old, old mansion. No one had set foot in it for years, though there were plenty of rumours going around about the place, I can tell you. It was meant to be haunted, you see. And on this particular night, we were working late . . .

'Must have been around midnight when things started going wrong. My mate Jack, he was up in the roof when a huge flying thing came swooping down from the rafters and took both his ears right off with one flap of its wings! Must have been a giant bat, we thought. Anyway, I wrapped poor Jack's ears up in my handkerchief and kept them for him. Here – have a feel!' And he passed round a couple of spongy things wrapped up in a cloth (which Lauren later discovered were pieces of dried apple).

As the story went on, poor Jack lost more and more of his body parts, which Mr Turner had thoughtfully kept for him and now passed around. Soon everyone was screaming delightedly as they dabbled their fingers in bowls of brains, blood, eyes and bones.

The thing is, that kind of story is so crazy everyone knows it can't be true, Lauren thought, trying to work out why her dad's creepy tale was so much less frightening than one of Sunny's.

You could easily imagine the horrific events in her stories really happening . . .

Sunny still hadn't arrived by the time the party was drawing to an end and most of the guests had gone home. 'Why don't you wait for her in your room while your father and I clear up here?' Mrs Turner suggested to Lauren, Jess, Caz and Michelle. 'I'm sure she won't be long, and you can start getting ready for bed.'

'OK, Mum,' Lauren said, giving her a hug. 'Thanks for everything! And you too, Dad. I've almost forgiven you for that dummy trick.'

Her father only gave a spine-chilling laugh in reply and chased everyone upstairs.

'I've had a fantastic time,' Caz said, helping Lauren drag a mattress out from under her bunk bed. 'This has been one of the best parties ever!'

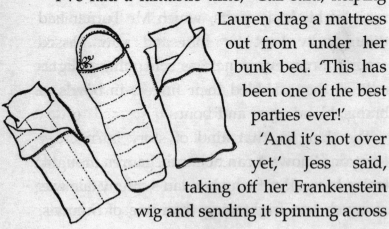

'And it's not over yet,' Jess said, taking off her Frankenstein wig and sending it spinning across the room. 'What shall we do now?'

'Well, we can't have any spooky stories till Sunny gets here,' Michelle said, 'so—'

'We're not having *any* spooky stories, full stop!' Lauren exclaimed. 'Remember what we promised my mum?'

'OK, so it's Truth or Dare!' Michelle shrugged. 'Bags I start first.'

Lauren went over to the window and began to draw her bedroom curtains. She took one last look at the cardboard tombstones, even spookier now the outside light had been switched off and they loomed out of the darkness. Fingers of mist curled around them. Lauren shivered. It could have been a real graveyard.

Suddenly, she caught her breath. She blinked, shook her head to clear it and looked again. No, she hadn't been imagining things! Near the end of the garden, a vague white shape was shimmering over the grass towards the house. It seemed to float rather than walk, arms (if they *were* arms) out-stretched. Now it had reached the gravestones, and passed straight through them without slowing down or wandering away from its steady course.

Party Girls

'Guys,' Lauren croaked, her mouth dry and her heart pounding out another drum roll. 'Come here, quick!'

This time, she didn't have the strength to scream. All she could do was point with a trembling finger at the pale figure coming closer and closer towards them . . .

'Wh-what do you think it is?' Jess whispered. The ghostly, shimmering form had come to a halt at the edge of the graveyard and was staring up at Lauren's bedroom window.

'And what does it want?' Michelle looked at the others, her eyes wide with terror. 'Seems like it's waiting for us!'

Caz only shook her head, too terrified to speak.

The figure raised both arms in the air, swaying a little from side to side, and the girls gradually became aware of a high-pitched, keening sound rising above the moaning wind.

Lauren's heart was still threatening to jump out of her chest but, having got over the initial shock, she was beginning to think more clearly now. Ghostly figures in white didn't really exist, did they, outside horror films? She forced herself to stare down at the figure in the garden. Well, if they *did* exist, they certainly didn't wear trainers! And hadn't she heard the wailing voice somewhere before?

'That's no more a ghost than I am!' she exclaimed, turning to the others. 'Can't you guess who it is? Listen!'

They strained to hear for a couple of seconds before exclaiming with one voice, 'Sunny!'

'Oh, she nearly gave me a heart attack!' Caz said, her shoulders sagging with relief.

'I knew all along it wasn't really a ghost,' Michelle added. 'But even so . . .'

'Oh, yeah?' Jess shot her a knowing glance. 'You looked scared enough just now.' She peered down into the garden with a gleam in her eye. 'Come on, let's get our own back! You and Caz stay at the window, Miche, so she doesn't suspect anything, and Lauren and I can creep down and ambush her.'

The lights were on downstairs and Lauren's parents were busy getting the house back to normal. So she and Jess crept through the kitchen and out into the garden. Now they were closer, it was easy to see the ghost was Sunny – shrouded in a length of pale cloth with her face painted white. Lauren couldn't believe she'd ever been taken in by the trick! Sunny was so busy with her act that she didn't notice them stealing towards her until it was too late to run away.

'Don't think you can fool us!' Jess shouted, wrestling her to the ground. 'We knew all along it was you!'

'It was a good trick though, wasn't it?' Sunny shrieked, in between giggles. 'Don't you think I looked spooky? Hey, stop tickling, Laurie!'

'But you're a ghost!' Lauren told her, her fingers searching for the most ticklish place under Sunny's arms. 'And ghosts can't feel anything, can they?'

'This one can!' Sunny was almost hysterical with laughter. 'Stop!'

By now, Caz and Michelle had piled down into the garden. Sunny managed to break away so they all chased her round the graveyard, giggling and shouting.

'What's going on?' Lauren's mother called from the back door. 'You should be upstairs getting ready for bed instead of rushing round the garden like a bunch of lunatics!'

'Sorry, Mum,' Lauren said breathlessly. 'But Sunny's just arrived.'

'Oh.' Valerie Turner looked surprised. 'I didn't hear her. Well, you must all come in right now, or Mrs Cooper'll be on the phone telling me what hooligans you are.'

'Sorry! It's my fault for being late,' Sunny said, as though butter wouldn't melt in her mouth. She picked up her rucksack and sleeping bag from behind one of the tombstones and trooped into the house with her friends. Lauren glanced quickly up at the dark windows of the next-door house as they went inside. Surely Mrs Cooper could let them have some fun tonight, of all nights?

'Oh no!' Sunny gasped as she looked down at herself under the bright kitchen lights. 'This is my mother's best funeral sari! She's going to kill me!' The fine white cotton was splattered with mud and streaked with vivid grass stains.

'Bring it back down when you've changed into your nightclothes and I'll see what I can do,' Valerie said. 'Now, upstairs – and calm down! Or this'll be the last sleepover for a long while.'

'We'll just have to keep the noise down,' Lauren told everyone when they were up in her bedroom again. 'Mum can't be expecting us to go to sleep straight away.'

'Then, as I was saying before we were so rudely interrupted,' Michelle said, sitting cross-legged on a mattress, 'Truth or Dare! What's it going to be, Sunny?'

After they'd gone through all the usual dares (gurgling a song through a mouthful of water, ringing Jess's brother Matt and saying you loved him, calling something stupid out of the front bedroom window) and some tricky truth questions (Have you ever weed in a swimming pool? Do you pick your nose? Have you lied to anyone in this room?), Jess suddenly turned to Lauren, who had chosen a dare for her turn.

'I've got a great one!' she said. 'This is your

party, so you have to do something really exciting. Go trick-or-treating at Mrs Cooper's house!'

'You must be joking!' Lauren replied. 'Call round there in the middle of the night? She'll eat me alive!'

'Of course she won't,' Jess said. 'Her bark's worse than her bite, if you ask me.'

'Besides, it's not the middle of the night,' Michelle added, glancing at the Snoopy clock on Lauren's bedroom wall. 'It isn't quite ten o'clock yet. Don't be such a wuss.'

Lauren looked back at her friends, wondering what to do. Sunny was making chicken noises, while Michelle and Jess exchanged knowing looks. 'Lauren's being a scaredy-cat, as usual,' was what they were saying to each other. Well, I'll show them, she decided, with a sudden mad rush of daring. For once in my life, I'm going to take a risk. That'll wipe the smiles off everyone's faces!

'OK,' she said casually, reaching for her dressing gown. 'I'll do it.' And she was delighted to see their jaws drop.

'We'll watch you from the front bedroom,' Sunny said, after a pause. 'No cheating!'

Caz followed Lauren through the bedroom door. 'Are you sure about this?' she whispered when they were out on the landing. 'You don't have to do it, you know. I wouldn't!'

Lauren hesitated, chewing her lip – but it was too late to back out now. 'Better get it over and done with,' she whispered back. 'See you later.'

'Just pretend to ring the bell,' Caz said hurriedly. 'No one'll know. Stand there for a few seconds with your arm up and then come back.'

Lauren nodded, her hand on the banister. Taking a deep breath, she began to creep downstairs.

Getting out of the house was surprisingly easy. Her parents were both in the living room, ready to watch the ten o'clock news on TV. Lauren could hear its signature tune as she tiptoed past down the hall. She walked quickly through the kitchen, then unlocked the back door and slipped through it into the garden. It seemed a much darker, more menacing place now that she was on her own.

Lauren made her way carefully round the back of the house to the side passage. Over the fence, she could see Caz's mum and stepdad chatting in their kitchen. Bending double so they wouldn't catch sight of her, she kept close to the wall as she stole along the narrow path. Why hadn't she thought to switch the outside light on first? It had been raining so much recently that the passage was damp and slippery. Yeuch! That was a deep puddle. Water slopped into her left slipper and trickled icily between her toes.

A couple more steps and she was at the side gate. Come on! Open, you stupid thing! Lauren muttered all sorts of threats under her breath as she tugged at the stubborn latch. She had to hurry: if there wasn't much going on in the world, her parents wouldn't bother to watch the second half of the news. What if they came upstairs and saw she wasn't there?

At last the gate gave way. She staggered backwards, took a deep breath, then crouched down again and scuttled along the passage, past the side window of their living room. Her parents never bothered to draw the curtain over that one. Made it! She straightened up at the corner of the house and stood still for a moment, hoping her heart would slow down to a more normal rhythm. The street was quiet and empty. One dim orange street lamp shone down on the familiar bulk of her dad's white van, parked by the curb.

Nearly there! Lauren told herself, trying to ignore the fact that the worst part of her mission was still to come. She had to walk round the front of their house in her dressing gown and slippers, stand on Mrs Cooper's doorstep for a few seconds (she'd given up all idea of actually ringing the bell, thanks to Caz's brilliant suggestion), and then retrace her steps all the way back again.

It had to be now or never. After a quick glance up and down the street to make sure no one was coming, Lauren summoned up all her courage and ran, as lightly and quickly as she could, along the pavement to Mrs Cooper's gate. As she pushed it open, she glanced quickly back at her house. Caz, Jess, Sunny and Michelle were standing in a huddle at the upstairs window, watching her, so she gave them a quick wave.

What am I doing here? she thought, stumbling a little on the steps up to Mrs Cooper's front door. What if some weirdo comes past in a car and snatches me? What if Mrs Cooper's lying in wait behind the door and pulls me in? Lauren had never been so scared in her whole life. She raised one arm and pretended to press the bell, staring down at her sodden slippers so she wouldn't have to face the stained-glass panel set in Mrs Cooper's door. There was no telling what she might catch sight of behind it.

That was odd! There were a couple of bottles of milk standing to one side of the porch. Lauren and her dad had a running joke about the way Mrs Cooper lay in wait for the milkman and grabbed her milk before he could make it back to his float. Maybe she'd gone away? The house certainly looked deserted – there wasn't a light on anywhere.

And then Lauren heard a strange noise on the

other side of the door. A distant, unearthly howling, like an animal in pain. She was about to rush back home in a blind panic – dare or no dare – when she suddenly realised what it was: Charlie was whining, somewhere in the house. With trembling fingers, she lifted the brass letter-box flap and peered through. What she saw in the hall made her even more certain something was wrong. A pizza delivery leaflet and a letter lay, undisturbed, on the doormat.

'Mrs Cooper? Are you all right?' she called timidly, her voice sounding unnaturally loud in the quiet night.

There was no reply.

'You must be mad. Stark raving bonkers!' Jess stared at Lauren in disbelief. 'Are you seriously thinking of going down to your parents and saying, "By the way, when I went out just now in the middle of the night on my own and rang on Mrs Cooper's bell, there was no reply. Do you think she's OK?"'

'I thought you said it wasn't very late when you gave me the dare!' Lauren scowled accusingly.

'That's because we never believed for one second that you'd actually do it,' Michelle said. 'Oh, Laurie, stop worrying! Mrs Cooper didn't answer the door when your mum went round to ask for Jess's ball either, did she? She's probably tucked up in bed, fast asleep.'

'But she always takes in her milk the minute it's delivered,' Lauren insisted. 'There are letters lying on the mat and I know she hasn't gone away because she'd never leave Charlie behind. Something *must* be wrong!'

After standing for a couple more seconds on Mrs Cooper's doorstep, wondering what to do, Lauren had eventually hurried back home. Her parents were still in the living room with the television on, so she raced past the door and upstairs to meet her friends on the landing. Now they were having a de-briefing session in her bedroom. So far, the feeling seemed to be that she should forget Mrs Cooper and count herself lucky for having got away with the dare.

Sunny didn't agree, though. 'I think you're right,' she said slowly. 'It sounds like something *is* wrong next door. But Jess is right, too – your parents are going to throw a wobbly if they find out you've been round there. How are you going to explain that away?'

Lauren sighed. She felt as though she'd already been brave enough to last a lifetime – summoning up the courage for a run-in with her parents might be a step too far. 'What do you think, Caz?' she asked.

Caz stopped chewing on a fingernail. 'It's difficult,' she replied. 'You probably will get into trouble if you own up. But imagine how you're going to feel if you don't say anything and something *has* happened to Mrs Cooper!'

Lauren realised that she'd known all along what had to be done. Now came the difficult part: actually doing it. She got up from the bed and pulled her dressing-gown belt more tightly around her waist. 'Wish me luck!' she said, trying to smile and almost succeeding as she headed for the bedroom door.

'You mean to tell us you've been roaming around the street on your own in your night-clothes? At this time of night? Lauren, what were you *thinking* of?' Mrs Turner's voice cracked in disbelief.

'Sorry, Mum.' Lauren shifted awkwardly from one foot to another and looked down at the floor. She felt so stupid, standing there in the middle of the room while her parents stared at her as though she'd gone insane.

'It was my fault.' Lauren turned around to find Jess standing there, with Michelle, Sunny and Caz lurking a few paces behind her in the doorway.

'We were playing Truth or Dare,' Jess went on, blushing bright red and twisting her fingers awkwardly together. 'I dared Lauren to go round to Mrs Cooper's.'

'We all told her to do it,' Sunny added.

'Not one of your brighter ideas, Jess,' Lauren's mum muttered, putting her mug of tea down on the table and getting up. 'Look, we'll have to talk about this later. I'd better go next door and see if anything really is wrong.'

'Shall I come with you?' her husband asked.

Valerie shook her head. 'Don't worry. Mrs Cooper knows me better than you, and she'll probably have a fit if she sees a man hammering at the door.'

'I'm really sorry, Dad,' Lauren repeated after her mother had left, slamming the front door behind her. 'I know it was a stupid thing to do.'

'Well, I suppose we've all done stupid things at one time or another,' he said. 'Come on, let's go and make some hot chocolate. No point in ordering you girls back to bed, is there? Not till we find out what's happening.'

When they were on their own in the kitchen, he laid both hands on Lauren's shoulders and asked, 'Why did you go through with such a mad idea, Laurie? It's not like you.'

'That's why I did it,' Lauren replied, meeting her father's eyes for the first time. 'I'm sick of everyone thinking I'm a wuss. The others are always doing crazy things and I wanted to show them I could be brave too. And myself, I suppose.' Funny, she hadn't thought of it like that before.

'Well, you've certainly done that,' Mr Turner said, pouring hot milk into mugs. 'I don't mean going next door, though. It probably took even more courage to own up to us about it. You did the right thing in the end, Lauren – I'm proud of you.'

'Thanks!' she replied, surprised.

'I'll say one last thing,' her father went on,

whisking up the chocolate. 'There's a difference between being scared because something's new and difficult, and being scared because it's dangerous. Some things are worth plucking up your courage for and some things aren't. Understand?'

'Yeah, Dad,' Lauren said, hanging her head again. It seemed so obvious now.

'Right, then help me carry these drinks through. Your mum'll probably come back any minute and tell us Mrs Cooper's dancing a jig in the living room!'

But when she did return a few minutes later, Valerie Turner looked serious. 'I think you're right,' she said. 'Something's not right at all. I'm going to ring the police straight away.'

'You don't think the old lady saw me dressed up as a ghost and had a heart attack, do you?' Sunny whispered to the others as they all waited in the living room.

'You weren't that convincing!' Jess told her, conveniently forgetting how spooked they'd been earlier.

'Just think!' Michelle told Lauren, her eyes wide. 'You might have saved Mrs Cooper's life! D'you think she's rich? She could leave you all her money when she dies and your life will be changed for ever.'

'Huh! I don't think so,' Lauren snorted. Somehow she couldn't imagine Mrs Cooper having a complete personality change. She was more likely to go spare at the idea of Lauren bothering her in the first place.

Mrs Turner went back outside to wait for the police to arrive, so Lauren's dad suggested watching a video to take their minds off things. They were all much too wound up even to think of going to sleep.

'Now, what have we got here?' he said, looking through the videos in the big cupboard under the TV. 'How about *Buffy the Vampire Slayer*?'

'No way, Dad,' Lauren groaned. 'Let's have *The Incredible Journey* instead.' They'd all had enough spooks and scares already that evening to last a lifetime!

* * *

'You write the next bit, Laurie,' Caz said, sliding out of the computer chair. 'After all, you were the big hero.'

'OK,' Lauren said, taking her place. She did feel quite proud of herself. One of the paramedics had told her mum that Mrs Cooper would certainly have died if she'd had to spend another night without help.

She was in bed with pneumonia, **Lauren told Nikki.** Apparently she'd been there since Saturday and no one had missed her. And if I hadn't gone round there last night, they never would have done either. Mum couldn't be too cross with me because I did save Mrs Cooper's life — the grumpy old bat. She told them at the hospital that if rang her doorbell again, she'd call the police. Can you imagine!

'Charlie!' Michelle giggled. 'Stop licking my ear! We'll take you to the park in a minute.'

Lauren smiled and carried on typing. 'Anyway, the best part of the whole thing is — guess what? We've got Mrs Cooper's dog to look after while she's in hospital, and that could be weeks! Do you remember? Charlie — we told you about him before. We're all really glad everything's working out for you — but we still miss you! How was Nancy's Hallowe'en party? Did you go trick-or-treating? Write and let us know!

She looked over at Sunny, Jess, Caz and Michelle. Heads close together, they were looking at a magazine spread out on the dining-room table. 'Your turn now, Sunny,' she said, getting up. 'You should be the one to tell her we're famous.'

At the end of the summer term, Sunny had won a competition in her favourite magazine. They'd all gone off to London to model party clothes for a photo shoot, and had been on tenterhooks ever since, waiting for the pictures to appear. And now here they were – splashed in full colour over the pages of *Girlgroove*!

Lauren took Sunny's place at the table and feasted her eyes on that super-cool picture of herself in a snakeskin skirt and a silver top, with a silver bandeau in her hair.

She didn't usually like seeing herself in photos – her hair always seemed to be in a mess or her mouth gaping wide open like a fish – but this was different. She looked fantastic! They all did, in fact. Nikki was standing next to her in a black strappy dress threaded with gold, and gold slides in her curly blonde hair.

'These pictures are so brilliant,' Michelle sighed, propping her chin on her hands and gazing at them rapturously. 'Look at us – born to boogie!'

'And it was all because of my birthday,' Caz said. 'If you lot hadn't thrown me such a brilliant surprise party, Sunny wouldn't have been able to write about it and win the competition.' She sighed happily. 'I still think that was the best party ever.'

'Hey, what about my disco?' Jess asked, putting an arm round her shoulder.

'And Nikki's farewell do,' Sunny added, taking her eyes off the computer screen for a second. 'Remember what a laugh that was?'

'But it was so sad when we had to say goodbye to her!' Lauren said, looking at the picture of Nikki and wishing with all her heart she was there to share the excitement.

'Now don't start getting gloomy on us,' Caz said gently, rubbing Lauren's back. 'Nikki won't be gone for ever, and we can do something really special to welcome her home again!'

'That's true,' Lauren admitted, cheering up.

What really mattered was the fact that the six of them would always be friends – there for each other no matter how far apart they were. And just think of all the amazing parties still to come!

If you'd like to throw a party like Lauren's read on . . .

GATHER ROUND, GHOSTS AND GHOULIES!

You can really go to town with a Halloween party. It's easy to turn your house into a spooky cavern – something as simple as changing the ordinary lightbulbs to coloured ones will cast an eerie glow. Most people enjoy making themselves look as ghoulish as possible, and freaky costumes don't have to be complicated – old clothes, spray-in hair dye and face paints may be all you need to become a scary zombie.

One word of warning: if you're going trick-or-treating, take an adult with you and only call on people you know. Your neighbours may not want to be disturbed!

Invitations

Haunted-house invitations look really effective. Start off by making a crooked house template out of card and cut one black and one orange house shape per invitation. Put the black shapes on a board and, using a craft knife and a ruler, carefully slit open a couple of windows with shutters. Cut two horizontal lines for the top and bottom of the window, and one vertical line down the middle so you can fold the shutters back, like this:

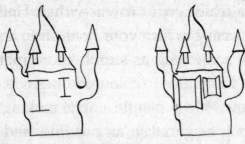

Write the party information on the orange card windows and decorate the outside of the houses with gold, silver or fluorescent pens. You can draw peeping eyes, spooky cats, cobwebs, bats and skulls. Or if you're not very artistic, just add some creepy stickers!

Pumpkin invitations are even simpler to make. Again, make a template from card and cut one black and one orange pumpkin shape per invite, as shown below. This time, put the orange shapes on a board and carefully

write here →

open

cut out the pumpkin faces with a craft knife and a ruler (you can probably do a couple of faces at a time). Stick the orange pumpkins on top of the black ones at the stalk and draw round the eyes, nose and mouth in pencil on the black card underneath so you can see where they are. Avoiding these areas, write your party information with a gold, silver or fluorescent pen.

Decorations

Pumpkin lanterns are a must at Hallowe'en. Put your pumpkin on a board and cut a slice off the top to make a lid. Scoop out the flesh inside until a thickness of about 2–3 cm is left and then carefully carve a face into the pumpkin skin (you might want to draw the outline in felt tip first, before you start cutting). Straight lines are easiest! Even a simple design looks stunning in the dark, with a night light burning inside.

Here are some other ideas to set the scary mood:

Balloon ghosts: Blow up a white balloon and tie a length of string around the knot so you can hang it up. Cut a square of thin white fabric or tissue paper, large enough to drape over the balloon and hang down below. Make a tiny hole in the centre of the material and place it over the top of the balloon, hooking through the string. Add some staring eyes with glow-in-the-dark fabric paint, or cut them out of black card and attach with double-sided tape. Hang your ghost from the ceiling or a light fitting.

Pipe-cleaner spiders: These spiders are very quick and easy to make if you can find some pressed cotton or styrofoam balls from a craft shop. Paint the balls black and carefully make four holes on each side with a metal skewer or the point of some scissors. Cut black pipecleaners in half and push one 'leg' into each hole, securing with a dab of glue if necessary. Bend the legs up into a curved shape and finish off with an upturned flick. Add a pair of googly eyes, then thread some string or elastic cord through the spider's body and hang him in a doorway or use him to decorate your table.

Haunted mansion: Cover the furniture in your house with sheets, so it looks as though no one has lived there for ages, and cover the windows with black crêpe paper, cut into tatters. Add vases of dried flowers, sprayed with black or silver paint, and see if you can get hold of any white wispy cobwebs from the Christmas decorations.

Silly graveyard: Cut some tombstone shapes out of card (you can use the sides of a cardboard box) and paint them grey – spray paint is quickest. Add some decorations with black marker pen and some jokey names or rhymes, then attach a short bamboo cane or stake to the back of each tombstone with brown parcel tape. Position them in your garden.

Pumpkin piñata

You'll need to start making this piñata a few days before your party. It can be messy, so wear an apron and roll up your sleeves! Tear lots of newspapers into strips and mix up some wallpaper paste according to the instructions on the packet. Blow up a balloon and tie a knot in the end, then soak each newpaper strip in paste and layer them all over the balloon. You will need about three or four complete layers of newspaper over the whole thing. Leave it to dry for a couple of days, then carefully cut a small hole in the top, prick the balloon (if it hasn't already popped) and pull it out. Make a couple of holes near the top of the piñata and thread through some string, to hang it up. Carefully push in the bottom, to make a flattish pumpkin base. Paint the piñata orange, adding eyes, nose and mouth with black marker pen when the orange paint is dry, and stick some long black and orange crêpe paper streamers around the bottom. Fill the piñata with sweets, hang it up and invite your party guests to take turns trying to break it with a stick – blindfolded first! (Make sure everyone else stands well back.)

Creepy costumes

There are lots of ideas for dressing up in this story, but here are a few more:

Bride of Dracula: Wear a long dress and perhaps a shawl and some elbow-length evening gloves, to look old-fashioned. Paint your face white and slip in some plastic vampire teeth. A trickle of fake blood down your chin completes the look.

'Thing': This is probably the easiest costume of all. Take a black dustbin bag and cut strips into it, working from the open end towards the closed end of the bag. Slip it over your head and finish off with a pair of dark glasses. (This outfit is particularly good if you're feeling shy or having a bad hair day. You may need someone to lead you around.)

Frankenstein: You can make a quick wig out of some old tights, card and black wool. Cut two strips of black card about 3cm wide from the side of an A3 sheet (or stick two A4 sheets together). Glue them on top of each other for strength, then fold into half and half again, and tape at the open end to give you a square shape. Try this on your head and adjust the fit if necessary. Reinforce at the corners by taping on shorter strips of cardboard.

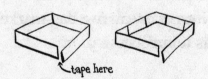

tape here

Cut a section about 25cm long from the leg of an old pair of tights, slitting it open to make a rectangular shape. Stretch this over your cardboard square, folding it over and taping to the card underneath to make the top of your wig. Cut lengths of black wool (as long as you want your 'hair' to be) and stick them to the underside of the wig with double-sided tape. Cut a fringe at the front.

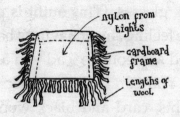

nylon from tights

cardboard frame

Lengths of wool.

To make bolts for your neck, cut a cork in half (with some adult help) and stick each half on to a small cardboard circle. Spray with gold or silver paint and, when they're dry, attach to each side of your neck with clear sticky tape.

Burglar: Hallowe'en costumes don't have to be scary. You can wear a stripy T-shirt and a black mask over your eyes, carry a bag marked 'Swag' and come as a burglar.

Tricky Treats

Ghost cake: You can make a cute little ghost out of three round sponge cakes. Lay them side by side, like a figure of eight, and trim off the sides to make a baby ghost shape. Make little 'arms' and a tail out of the third cake, like this:

Cover the whole shape in white ready-made icing, or make your own from icing sugar and lemon juice (it will need to be fairly thick). Add some eyes, eyebrows and a mouth made out of an unrolled liquorice wheel.

Ice-cream pumpkins: This idea for a sweet treat is based on the idea of pumpkin lanterns. Cut a lid off the top of an orange and – with some adult help, as this can be tricky – hollow out all the flesh inside, using a knife to start you off.

(Once you've peeled away some, you may find the rest comes easily.) When the orange is completely empty inside, carefully cut out a face as you did with the pumpkins, then fill the shell with vanilla, lemon or orange ice cream. Put the filled oranges back in the freezer until the party, but transfer them to the fridge an hour or so before you're ready to eat so that they soften a little.

Ghoulish Games

The Greasy Hand Game: This is rather like 'It', but with a creepy difference. The person who is trying to catch the others has a thick layer of Vaseline all over her hand. She's let loose in a darkened room or outside in the garden and has to grease everyone else!

Murder in the Dark: This one is an old favourite. One person is chosen to be the detective and leaves the room. While she's out, the others choose a murderer. Then they sit in a circle and invite the detective back into the room. The lights are turned out and the murderer has to get up and tap one of the others in the circle. That person screams and pretends to die – the lights go on and the detective has to guess who the murderer is. While she is trying to do so, the murderer has to wink secretly at the other players in turn, who must then also pick their moment to scream and die. The detective has to discover who the murderer is before everyone is dead!

PARTY GIRLS
Jennie Walters

All Hodder & Stoughton books are available at your local bookshop or newsagent, or can be ordered direct from the publisher. Just tick the titles you want and fill in the form below. Prices and availability subject to change without notice.

Hodder & Stoughton Books, Cash Sales Department, Bookpoint, 39 Milton Park, Abingdon, OXON, OX14 4TD, UK. E-mail address: orders@bookprint.co.uk. If you have a credit card you may order by telephone – (01235) 400414.

Please enclose a cheque or postal order made payable to Bookpoint Ltd to the value of the cover price and allow the following for postage and packing:
UK & BFPO: £1.00 for the first book, 50p for the second book and 30p for each additional book ordered up to a maximum charge of £3.00.
OVERSEAS & EIRE: £2.00 for the first book, £1.00 for the second book and 50p for each additional book.

Name . . . .

Address . . . .

. . . .

. . . .

If you would prefer to pay by credit card, please complete:
Please debit my Visa / Access / Diner's Club / American Express (delete as applicable) card no:

Signature . . . .

Expiry Date . . . .

If you would NOT like to receive further information on our products please tick the box. ☐